# Sweet as Sugar

Written by Oakley Graham

Illustrated by Kimberley Barnes

**TOP THAT**

Licensed exclusively to Top That Publishing Ltd
Tide Mill Way, Woodbridge, Suffolk, IP12 1AP, UK
www.topthatpublishing.com
Copyright © 2016 Tide Mill Media
All rights reserved
0 2 4 6 8 9 7 5 3 1
Manufactured in China

ISBN 978-1-78445-588-0

A catalogue record for this book is available from the British Library

For Bodhi, who is sweet as sugar - OG.

Once there was a young sugar glider who lived happily in a cosy nest with her mummy, daddy, brothers and sisters. However, the time came when it was time for her to move out of the family tree.

'It's time for you to find your own way in the world,' said her mummy, proudly.

The young sugar glider wasn't at all sure how to find her way in the world. But she tried to be brave, kissed her mummy on the cheek, and scampered on her way.

The young sugar glider scurried from tree to tree, looking for a safe place to make her first nest. At last, she came across a tall tree, with a large hole in its trunk.

'An ideal home!' she thought.

After lots of hard work, the young sugar glider had built a very fine nest indeed.

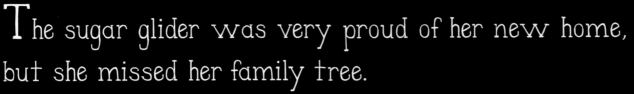

The sugar glider was very proud of her new home, but she missed her family tree.

There was no mummy to stroke her fur when she woke up, no daddy to bring her a sweet nectar treat for supper, and no brothers and sisters to groom and play with.

For the first time in her life,
the young sugar glider
was all alone.

Nearby, there lived a family of brushtail possums.

Mummy Possum had been keeping an eye on the young sugar glider, and seeing that she was upset, invited her to dinner. Although the young sugar glider was upset, she was also VERY hungry!

First she ate Mummy
Possum's entire store of
flower nectar.

Then she ate all of
Mummy Possum's honey.

HONEY

'You sure have a sweet tooth,'
said Mummy Possum, smiling.
'From now on, I'm going to call
you Sugar!'

Sugar grew to like her new home and loved playing with her brushtail possum neighbours. But she didn't like it when the possum babies teased her about being different.

'You've got leftover skin,' they all laughed.

'They're right. Why do I have so much skin anyway?'
wondered Sugar sadly.
Sugar wished more than anything to be
just like her friends.

One day, Sugar was woken from her sleep
by a strange smell in the forest.

Suddenly, the calm was broken as animals,
big and small, stampeded past.

Wondering what the animals could be running from,
Sugar quickly climbed to the treetop and saw a ...
BUSHFIRE!

The bushfire was moving fast and destroying everything in its path.

Before Sugar had time to warn Mummy Possum and her family about the danger, the fire was crackling all around, and they were trapped!

Without thinking, Sugar launched herself from the branches of the tree and spread out her legs and arms.

The skin the possum cubs had
teased her about acted like the
wings of a glider, and Sugar soared
over the fire to safety!

'So that's why I'm different!'
shouted Sugar excitedly.

Now Sugar had to find help for Mummy Possum!
Jumping and gliding from tree to tree she spied a
herd of kangaroos in the distance.

'Help! Help!' Sugar yelled. 'There's a fire in the
forest and my friends are trapped!'

The kangaroos heard Sugar's calls for help and
followed her back into the burning forest.

The kangaroos bounded back and forth, back and forth, using their enormous feet to stamp out the flames. Soon, the bushfire was under control and Mummy Possum and her family were safe!

Sugar had saved her friends and had found her own way in the world all in one amazing day.

She had also learnt an important lesson ...

Sugar now knows that it is good
to be different after all!